The Messy Book

ILLUSTRATED BY
Jean Smit

STORY WRITTEN BY
Wendy Robertson

You are loved just the
way you are
♡ Wendy

www.messy-life.com
wendy@messy-life.com

Tellwell Talent
www.tellwell.ca

ISBN
978-0-2288-0465-9 (Hardcover)
978-0-2288-0464-2 (Paperback)

The Messy Book is fiction but it is based on the author's life growing up. Everyone from four and ninety-four years of age will enjoy this book because we are all children at heart who need to be loved for who we are. This book is written as an encouragement for everyone who messes up – which is all of us!

Special thanks to the author's brother, Bruce Grierson, and friend, Sharon Kisilevich for their help with editing. Bruce helped edit the initial stages of the book and has himself authored the books *U-Turn*, published by Bloomsbury, and *What Makes Olga Run?* published by Random House Canada. Sharon Kisilevich adopted this book as her own and spent many hours with the author on revisions.

The author dedicates this book to all who have walked with her on her healing journey, specifically the team of Ellel Ministries and the teachers of Father Heart Ministries:
www.ellel.org/ca-ab/
www.fatherheart.net

One day I made a **mess** and Momma scolded me.
So, I believed "Mess" was bad! "Neat" was what I needed to be.

It all seemed so unfair because "mess" was such fun,
To explore with paints and colours, mixing
green and blue in one.

The next day Momma called my name,
"Amy, I have a surprise for you!
Our family is going to the Club,
And you are coming too."

"Exchange your drawings
and your paints,
To play tennis
and other sports."
My heart said,
"What I like is wrong,
And I
mess-up
on the court."

I do what they don't understand.
I'm not who they think I should be.
I have no interest in sports.
Was I born into the wrong family?

That night I found
Momma's lipstick.
I'll leave a note
for her to see.
I'll draw a heart
on the bathroom mirror,
She will be
SO proud of me!

In my neatest printing I wrote,

"Luv you Momma"

with a heart in red!
Then much too excited to go to sleep,
I lay awake for a while in my bed.

Next morning, I ran to the mirror,
But the note with the heart was gone,
Momma had wiped it all clean,
My tummy turned upside down.

"She must be angry with me, even though I drew my best."
Again, my heart spoke loud and clear. It said,

"I am the mess!"

I believed my parents would love me if I put away my art.
But a sad thing happened when I did, I closed a part of my heart.

The next morning Momma said,
"You're dressed-up, so don't make a mess.
And please, Amy, please,
Don't get dirt on your dress!"

I ran outside to the garden,
I thought I'd take a look,
As I leaned to pick a flower,
That was all it took...

My shoe **caught** on my hem,
Down I went on hands and knees.

Then in my heart I saw **Jesus**,
I no longer felt out of place.
He smiled as He took the mud off of me,
And placed it on His face.

I heard His gentle whisper, "Amy, I'm not angry with you.
Others see only the mess that you've made,
but I see what's really true."

"I see you.
I know you.

I love you!

Be who I made you to be.
You are special, my
Amy, so beautiful.
You're made in the
likeness of Me!"

I laughed out loud and began to **paint**, and God was next to me.

All along I've been calling it wrong. But now He was setting me free!

My heart that was closed peaked open,
God's **comfort** poured through the door.
I used to think I was "The Mess",
But I don't believe that anymore.

I'm sorry Momma
that I didn't see
You did the best
you knew how.
"God, thank you for
making me as You did.
I like who
I am now!"

I climbed out of the box where I'd lived,
Humming a little song.

Soon the world seemed **big** and **scary**,
I needed a place to belong.

I sat on the ground feeling all alone,
And then I began to cry.

Until I saw **Jesus** reaching for me,
And He wiped the tears from my eyes.

As He swung me around I looked in His face,
Then asked, "Where can I be *me?*"

With joy in His smile, He took my hand,
And simply said,

"Come and you'll see!"

The Rest of the Story...

The end is just the beginning!

Just as Jesus takes Amy's hand so He invites all of us to join with
Him on a journey of discovering how much we are loved.

He is a Father who calls us His children and sent
His Son, Jesus, to reveal His love to us.

Let the adventure begin!

CPSIA information can be obtained
at www.ICGtesting.com
Printed in the USA
LVHW05n2154051018
592607LV00002B/4/P